The Fairy Clause?

Written by
Bud Geissler
Illustrated by
Joe Glemba

G 2 G Enterprises, LLC
Irwin, PA

The Fairy Clause

Did anyone
get the name
of that plane?

ISBN 978-0-578-13123-8

First Printing October 2013

Book Design by Joseph Glemba
Edited by Michelle Geissler

To Traye and Molly, you are my gifts from God.

To Michelle, you married a dreamer. Thanks for making them come true!

B.G.

To Tanya for her love, support and much needed feedback.

To Aniston, who brings so much joy into my life.

Last but not least. To Baba and Chai for making me laugh every day.

J.G.

The snow fell softly that cold winter's night. Traye's family sat down for a meal.
He had no idea the trouble he'd cause, you can check , this story is real!
It was dinner time and all was still well, Traye feasted on ham and some fries.
It wasn't his food but his choice of dessert that changed how Santa would fly!

Traye! Hurry up!
It's your turn to run the train!

This is the story of one taffy stick and one little five year old boy~who on Christmas Eve, though it wasn't his fault, almost cost you your toys
Traye got his snack, a sweet taffy stick, and that's what he started to chew.
But as everyone knows, with a loose tooth, this is not a good thing to do.

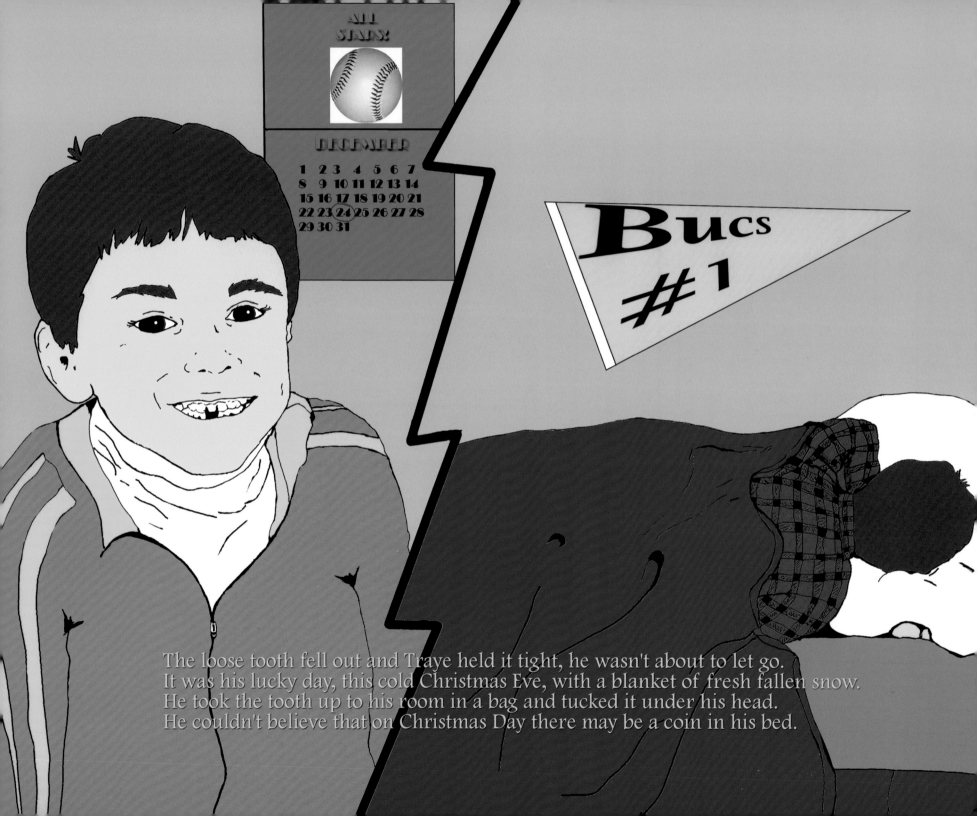

The loose tooth fell out and Traye held it tight, he wasn't about to let go.
It was his lucky day, this cold Christmas Eve, with a blanket of fresh fallen snow.
He took the tooth up to his room in a bag and tucked it under his head.
He couldn't believe that on Christmas Day there may be a coin in his bed.

Now the Tooth Fairy's busy most of the year, but tries to relax holidays.
What with all of the toys and stuff Santa brings, a coin can just get in the way.
But Traye tucked his tooth under his pillow and smiled up into the sky.
The Tooth Fairy knew what she had to do and so she started to fly.

...I know its Christmas Eve...
I have to work...

Now remember it is Christmas Eve and it's
someone else's big night.
Santa was working as fast as he could to get his
job done just right.
Out of the north the big man appeared with his
reindeer attached to his sleigh.
From the southeast the Tooth Fairy came to
deliver the coin to young Traye.

Both focused hard on the job to be done,
neither one of them looked around.

Santa's sleigh clipped the Tooth Fairy's wing and both of them crashed to the ground.

The Tooth Fairy's dust fell all over Claus, as he lay flat on his back.
And the Tooth Fairy smashed into our front door and landed on Santa's sack.
Then they got up and looked at each other, stunned and a little confused.
Santa picked up the glittering wand, the one that the Tooth Fairy used.
The Tooth Fairy brushed the snow from her face and flung Santa's bag on her back.
What just happened here, is what history says, threw that Christmas way out of whack!

Santa waved the wand to enter Traye's house and placed
a coin under the tree.
He continued on task for the rest of the night, and
finished at 5:53.

The Tooth Fairy, still holding Santa's big bag, was dazed from the mid-air mishap.
She placed Christmas toys under Traye's pillow as he took his long winter's nap.

She finished her work on that long Christmas Eve, then returned home for some sleep.
She stumbled in, exhausted, and fell into bed when she heard her cell phone beep.
It was Santa Claus~he was very upset! They had gotten everything mixed!
She saw that she had his bag in her room and it was too late to be fixed.

.....H..E...L..L..O....?

The sun came up on that Christmas morn and Traye was the first to arise.
I don't have to tell you his neck was quite stiff from his Tooth Fairy/Santa suprise.
Many children arose to gifts in their beds and coins left under the tree.
No one could fathom why this would occur, but Traye knew what it could be.

Worried that something went wrong at his house, Traye ran outside to the yard.
He could see where Santa Claus fell to the ground and knew that he had hit hard.
The marks on the door where the Tooth Fairy hit were unbelievable too.
The pile of pixie dust left at the scene turned out to be a great clue.

Traye surveyed the scene, wondering if the two magical guests were alright.
Would he be the only child whose presents got mixed-up that night?
Later that day it was all on the news, the Tooth Fairy/Santa flip flop.
No one complained they just wondered why and hoped next year it would stop.

**Tooth Fairy
Santa flip flop jobs!
Details at noon!**

That spring, after things quieted down, a letter
arrived for our Traye.
He opened it slowly... and wondered who
mailed it ... and just what the letter might say.

"Dear Traye," it started as most letters do and then it continued on.
"So glad that you kept our secret this year... you know, what went down on your lawn.
We had a small problem with our Christmas Eve flights, we got our magic confused,
The Tooth Fairy and I were a little mixed-up and saw ourselves on the news.
No need to worry, the problem is solved and now our flight paths are clear.
We are tracking ourselves on radar to avoid a mess next year."

Traye smiled and thought of all that occured as he chewed on some candy comb honey.
"Mom", he yelled as he pulled out a tooth,
"Can you call the Easter Bunny?"

Dear Traye,

This letter is in regards to last years mix-up. I would like to assure you that the Newest Model Santa Sleigh is one of the most technologically advanced models ever released. We have upgraded to an Air Ride suspension. We've added nine air bags. Seven are in the cockpit and two are in gift storage. A five point harness was installed to protect the Boss. In addition to our standard NKAS (Naughty Kid Avoidance System) and NKGPS (Nice Kid GPS), I have personally developed, the FRD (Fairy Radar Detection). The FRD has an impressive one hundred mile detection radius and is accurate to one inch. We at the Office of Sleigh Maintenance and Design feel that these additions will enable us to avoid any future embarrassment. We have enclosed a picture of our new facility. You may notice our cutting edge machinery and diagnostic equipment. We spared no expense. Santa also made sure we included a %50 off coupon for use at any Santa Inc. related business.

Sincerely,

Jim E. Elfton
Chief Officer OSMD

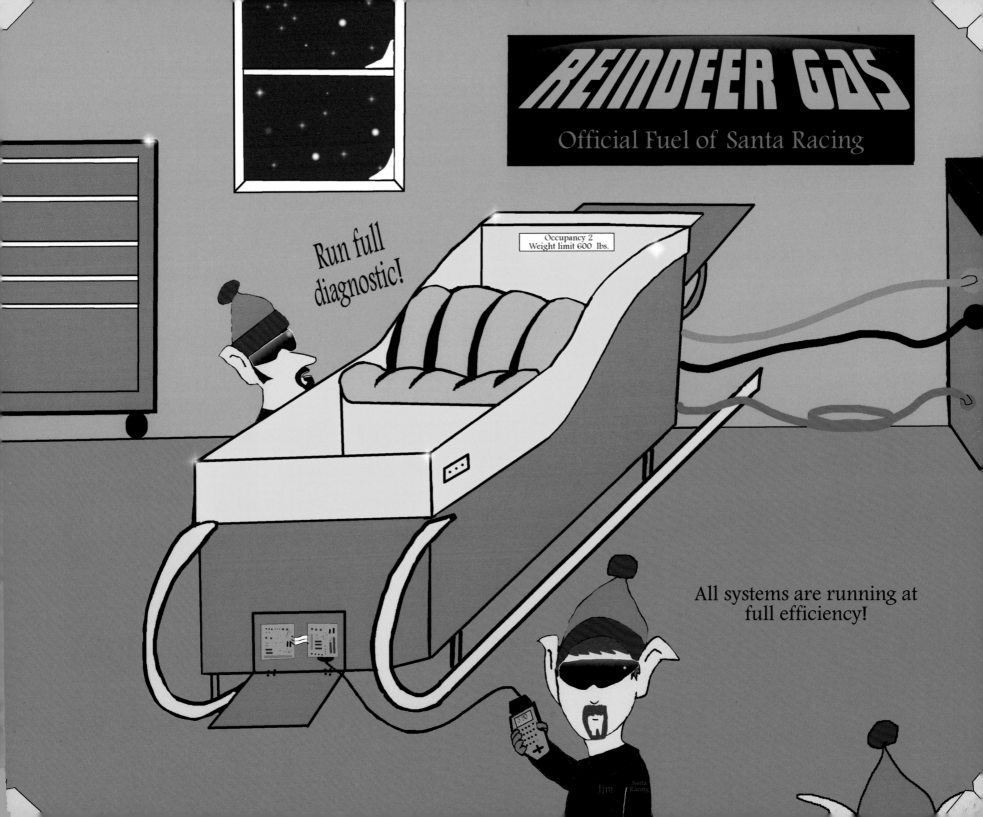

What People are saying about The Fairy Clause

"It is a nice fictional story. However, the likelihood of Santa's sleigh getting into an accident is impossible."

Jim E Elfton
Chief Officer OSMD

"I've lost 6 teeth so far and Dad hasn't written a book about me."

Traye's sister Molly

"If you read one book about Santa and the Tooth Fairy this year, make it this one!"

Mr. Good Taste

"Some of the best art I've ever seen!"

90 year old man who can't find his glasses

"The Tooth Fairy is gorgeous! She should be in movies."

Ms. T. F. Airy